To Noah ....

with a heart
full of love

Alex

Love is all around Georgia

Published by Sourcebooks Jabberwocky, an imprint of Sourcebooks, Inc.
P.O. Box 4410, Naperville, Illinois 60567-4410
(630) 961-3900
Fax: (630) 961-2168
www.sourcebooks.com

Source of Production: Worzalla, Stevens Point, Wisconsin
Date of Production: November 2016
Run Number: 5008152
Printed and bound in the United States of America.
WOZ 10 9 8 7 6 5 4 3 2

Love is all around Georgia

Written by Wendi Silvano

Illustrated by Joanna Czernichowska

sourcebooks
jabberwocky

Love is a feeling that comes from inside.

Everyone feels it. It can't be denied.

But how do we know that it's there? What's the clue?

How can we see it?

Just what can we do?

Love's all around, if you just pay attention,

in people and places too many to mention.

Go look at the **park,**

on the **street,**

at the **mall.**

You'll see love all over. It's **big** and it's small!

All around Georgia, in cars and on trains, in taxis and buses, on boats and on planes, in Roswell, Columbus, and Valdosta too, you'll find there is love that will come into view.

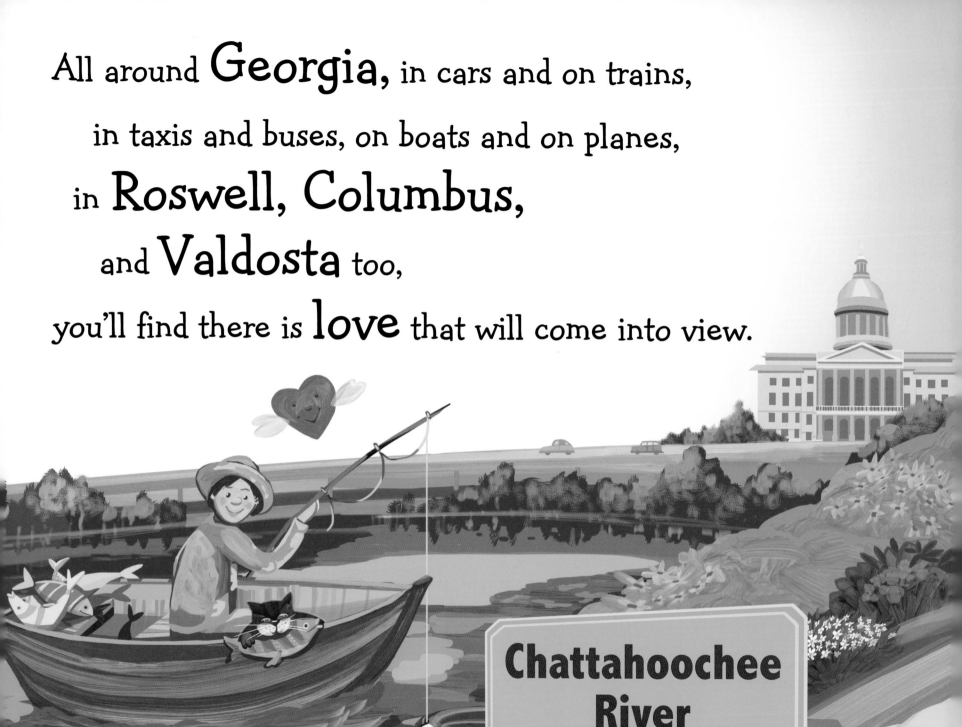

Chattahoochee River

Right there, on the lawn, in grand **Piedmont Park**

is a **mom** with her **babe,**

hearing songs of a lark.

Piedmont Park

She **swaddles** him, **cuddles** him,
kisses his ear.

That surely is **love,**
it's perfectly clear!

At a store in Atlanta, a girl gets a bear.
She squeezes him,
squishes him,
ruffles his hair.

It's clear that she **loves** him. She's **smiling** and bright.
She tucks him in **softly** and **gently** at night.

That same little girl, the very next day,

sees a **friend** at her school who is too **sad** to play.

So she sits down beside him and **listens** and **shares,**
making sure that he knows there's someone who **cares.**

Now the boy who was sad feels much better, you see,
so he runs home all happy to play with Magee.

They romp and they frolic.

They fetch and they run.

It's certain he loves him. They're having such fun!

You can see how **love** travels

when **shared** with a friend.

If *everyone* shares love, it never will end.

From one to another, it s p r e a d s and it **grows**.

You can't have *too much*, as everyone knows.

An officer in Savannah who **helps** change a flat.

A fireman in Athens who **rescues** a cat.

PHILIPS ARENA

The home team that makes the crowd **cheer** and **clap**.
Each moment has **love** like a **gift** you unwrap.

There's a **father** who sits at the table each night,
helping out with the homework to get it just **right**.

He's tired and busy, but that's **love**, you know…
giving up what you want to **help** someone else **grow**.

It's not only *people* who show love, it's true.

Just come see the creatures

that play at the zoo!

The polar bear tumbles

and rolls with her cub,

and when they are finished,

she gives him a rub.

Where else is there **love?** Have we looked all around?

I think we've forgotten—love grows from the ground!

In the **meadows** and **gardens** and parks you will find

that the earth shows us **love** of all shapes and all kinds.

Wherever you look, **love** comes into sight.

It's there in the morning, it's there in the night.

But in the whole state of **Georgia,**

the best love you'll find

is a **love** that is **gentle,**

and **selfless,** and **kind...**

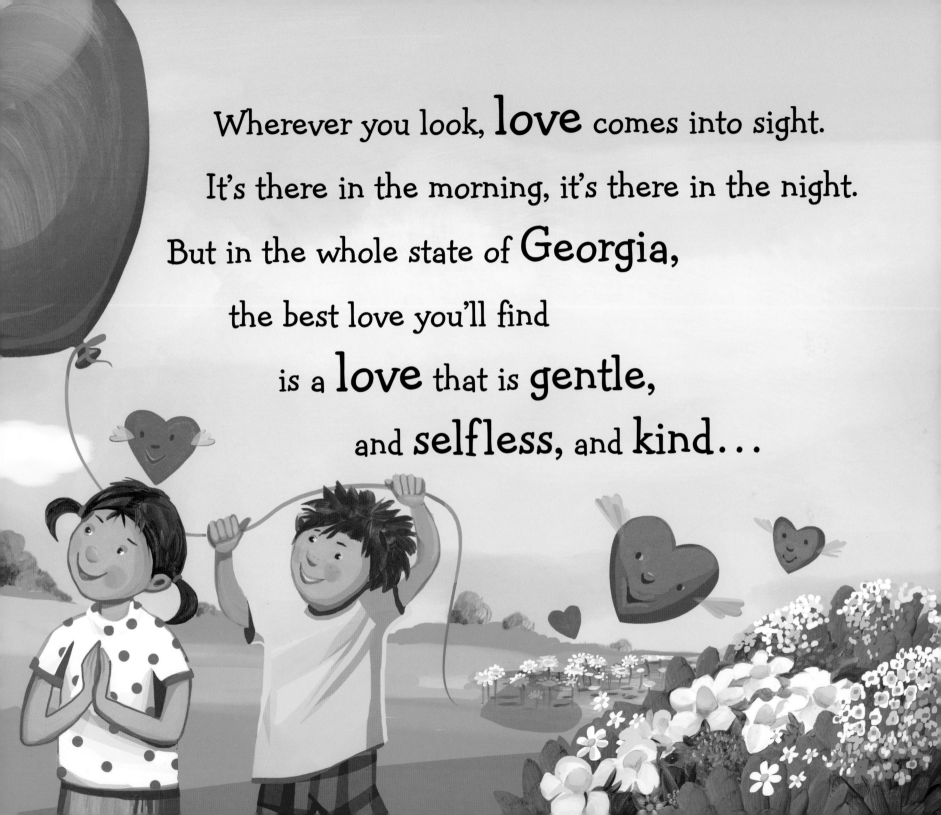

It's the love found at home. It shows up each day
in things people do and in things people say.
There's no greater love, I can tell you, it's true,
than the love of your family...

Especially for YOU!